This book belongs to

_____

For Paul and Rachael
—T.S.

For Rick and Faythe
—A.B.

Library of Congress Cataloging-in-Publication Data is available.

2 4 6 8 10 9 7 5 3 1

Published by Sterling Publishing Co., Inc. 387 Park Avenue South, New York, NY 10016

Text copyright © 2004 by Teddy Slater
Illustrations © 2004 by Aaron Boyd

Designed and produced for Sterling by COLOR-BRIDGE BOOKS, LLC, Brooklyn, NY

Distributed in Canada by Sterling Publishing
c/o Canadian Manda Group, One Atlantic Avenue, Suite 105
Toronto, Ontario, Canada M6K 3E7
Distributed in Great Britain and Europe by Chris Lloyd at Orca Book Services,
Stanley House, Fleets Lane, Poole BH15 3AJ, England
Distributed in Australia by Capricorn Link (Australia) Pty. Ltd.
P.O. Box 704, Windsor, NSW 2756, Australia

Printed in China
All rights reserved

Sterling ISBN 1-4027-1979-5

Black Cat Creeping

A Lucky Cat Story

by Teddy Slater • Illustrated by Aaron Boyd

Sterling Publishing Co., Inc.
New York

Black cat creeping on
Halloween night,
prowling down the alleyway,
green eyes bright.

Suddenly, two ghosts glide by,
pale beneath the dark night sky.

A fairy princess floats between
a frog prince and a jeweled queen.

Beasties dance and beasties sing.

What's that scary, hairy thing?

A pirate, a dragon, a clown appear!
A ghoul and goblin gather near.

Off they go, across the street,
marching to a ghostly beat.

A lonely witch
brings up the rear.

The pace picks up.
They're almost there.

A door creaks open. Come on in. . . .

The Halloween party's about to begin.

A fiddler plays a lively tune,
beneath a golden harvest moon.
Everybody whirls and twirls. . . .

Except the little witchy girl.

Apples bobbing in a tub.
Try to get one.
Glub, glub, glub!

The clock strikes nine.
The guests go home.

But now the witch is not alone.